David Walliams

PRESENTS...

For beautiful Wallis x

D.W.

For Wendy

T.R.

First published in hardback by HarperCollins *Children's Books* in 2017

This paperback edition published in 2019

HarperCollins *Children's Books* is a division of HarperCollins *Publishers* Ltd.

Text © David Walliams 2017. Illustrations © Tony Ross 2017

Cover lettering of author's name © Quentin Blake 2010

David Walliams and Tony Ross assert the moral right to be identified as the author and illustrator of the work.

A CIP catalogue record for this title is available from the British Library.

1 London Bridge Street, London SE1 9GF.

1 3 5 7 9 10 8 6 4 2

Printed and bound in Italy

978-0-00-817278-7

BOOGIE

BEAR

HarperCollins *Children's Books*

Illustrated by the artistic genius

Tony Ross

Up at the North Pole polar bears were
swimming, fishing and growling.

The biggest, furriest one of all was sunning
herself on an iceberg as usual.

Lying there without a care in the world, she scooped fish from
the sea with her paw and dropped them into her mouth.

"This is the life," she sighed
as she drifted off to sleep.

"ZZZZ...ZZZZ...ZZZZ...ZZZZ...

ZZZZ...ZZZZ...ZZZZ...ZZZZ...ZZZZ...Z

ZZZZ." When the polar bear finally woke up,

ZZZZ…ZZZZ…ZZZZ…ZZZz…

ZZZ…ZZZz…zzzz…ZZZZ…ZZZz…ZZZz…

the most awful thing had happened.

The animal must have eaten
too much for lunch again because the part of
the iceberg she was lying on had snapped off, and

floated

away.

The polar bear was now **miles** from home
and being **hurled** around by the angry sea.

"Oh dear,
oh dear,"

she said as she

wobbled,
surfing a
humongous
wave.

Surely things couldn't get any worse.

They could.

Much worse.

As the polar bear was
swept south, the sea became
warmer
and **warmer,**

melting the iceberg,
which became smaller
and smaller.

🐾 Free
geography
lesson.

Soon it was **no** bigger
than an ice cube.

"Oh dear, oh dear,
oh dear!"
said the polar bear as she
toppled over into
the sea.

Splosh!

Bobbing her head up out of the water, the polar bear spied that the nearest land was miles away.

"Oh dear, oh dear, oh dear, oh dear!"

She did her best **bear paddle** towards it, before collapsing on the rocks, waves crashing around her.

🐾 Bear paddle is like doggy paddle, but more beary.

Behind her she heard a **rustling** in the forest.

Rustle!

Rustle!

Rustle!

The only thing more rustley would be someone called Russell Russell rustling.

Looking up, the polar bear saw hundreds of eyes
staring back at her out of the gloom.
"Oh dear,

oh dear, oh dear,

oh dear, oh very dear!"

she whispered to herself.

Surely things couldn't get any worse.

They could.

Much worse.

"Charge!" came a voice.

Before the polar bear knew it, a hundred brown, furry creatures were stampeding towards her.

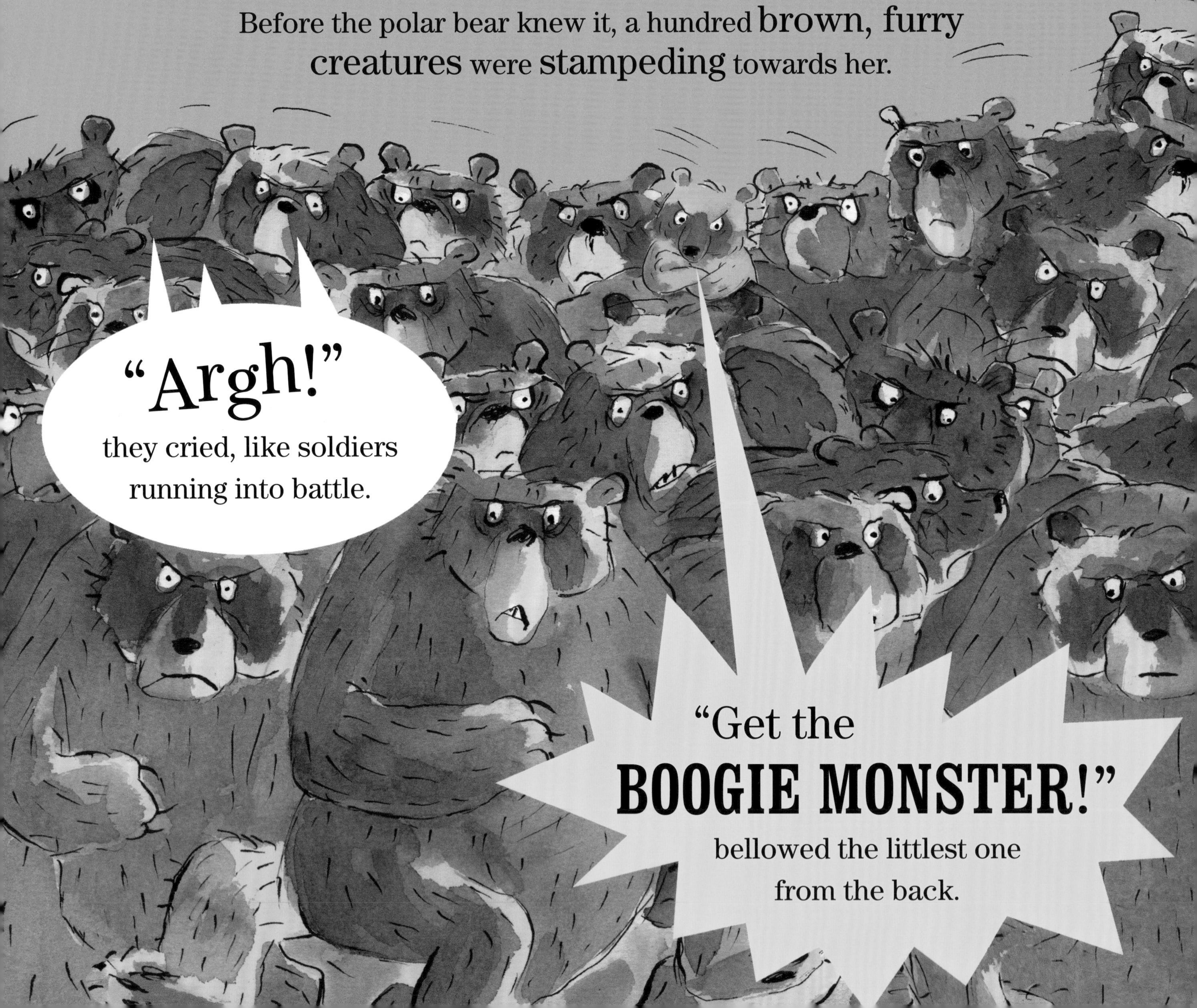

"Argh!" they cried, like soldiers running into battle.

"Get the **BOOGIE MONSTER!**" bellowed the littlest one from the back.

"Oh dear,
oh dear, oh dear, oh dear,
oh very **very** dear!"
said the polar bear,
and she **ran** away into the forest
as **fast** as she could.

🐾 It wasn't actually that fast, but at least she tried.

Brown bears came from all sides,
and soon the white bear had **nowhere** to run.

Ahead of her was the
tallest tree in the forest,
so she **clambered**
all the way **up**
to the **top**.🐾

🐾 It is impossible to clamber all the way up to the bottom.

The tree swayed
under her weight.

The white bear clung on desperately,
as the brown bears circled.

"Oh dear, oh dear,

oh dear, oh dear,

oh very, very extremely dear!"

she said to herself.

"Get the
BOOGIE MONSTER!"
shouted the small one, baring his sharp teeth.

"Can someone else do it?
It's scary!"
whined the one with the
biggest, wettest nose.

"I am **not scary!**"

shouted the polar bear.

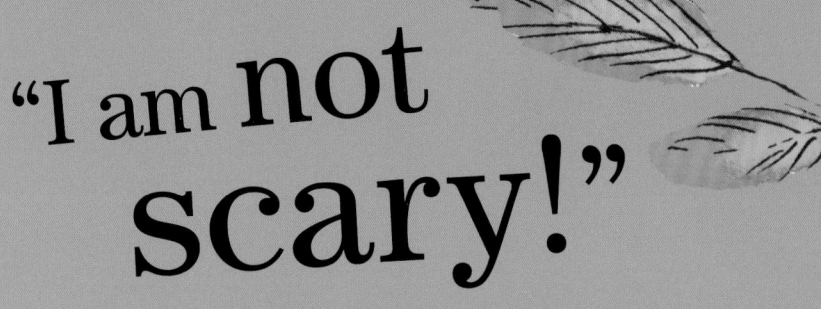

"Yes you are!"
said the little one.
"Your fur is a funny colour!"

"Well, I think your fur is a funny colour!"

That enraged him.

"Get UP there!"
he ordered.

"I'm scared of heights,"
replied the one with the
biggest, wettest nose.

The smallest one **huffed** and picked up a **stick** as **big** as he was.

He **hurled** it at the polar bear.

"Take THAT, BOOGIE MONSTER!"

Woosh!

Biff!

"Ouch!"
called out
the polar bear.

She lost her grip

and slid

down

the tree

at speed . . .

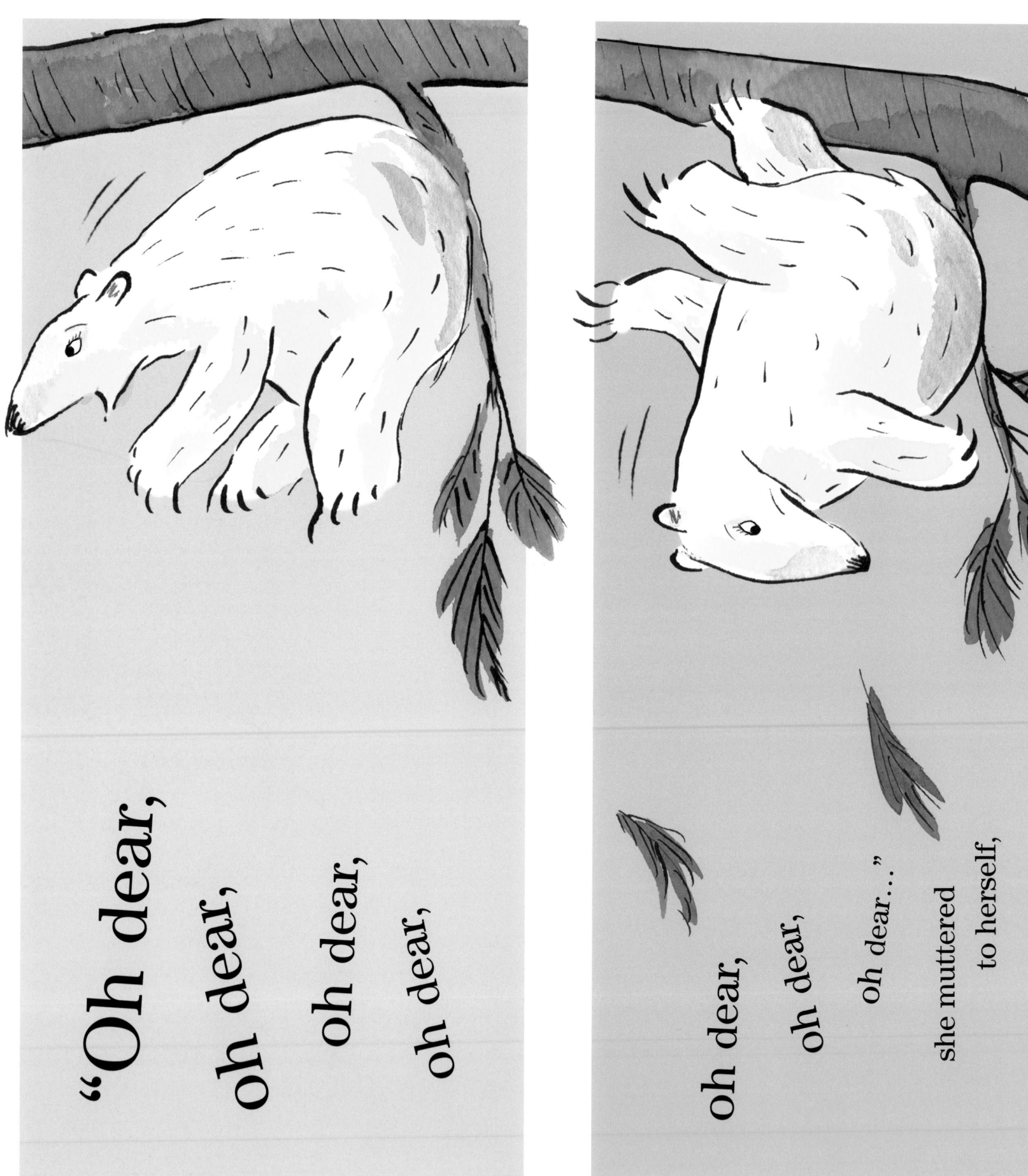

"Oh dear,
oh dear,
oh dear,
oh dear,

oh dear,
oh dear,
oh dear…"
she muttered
to herself,

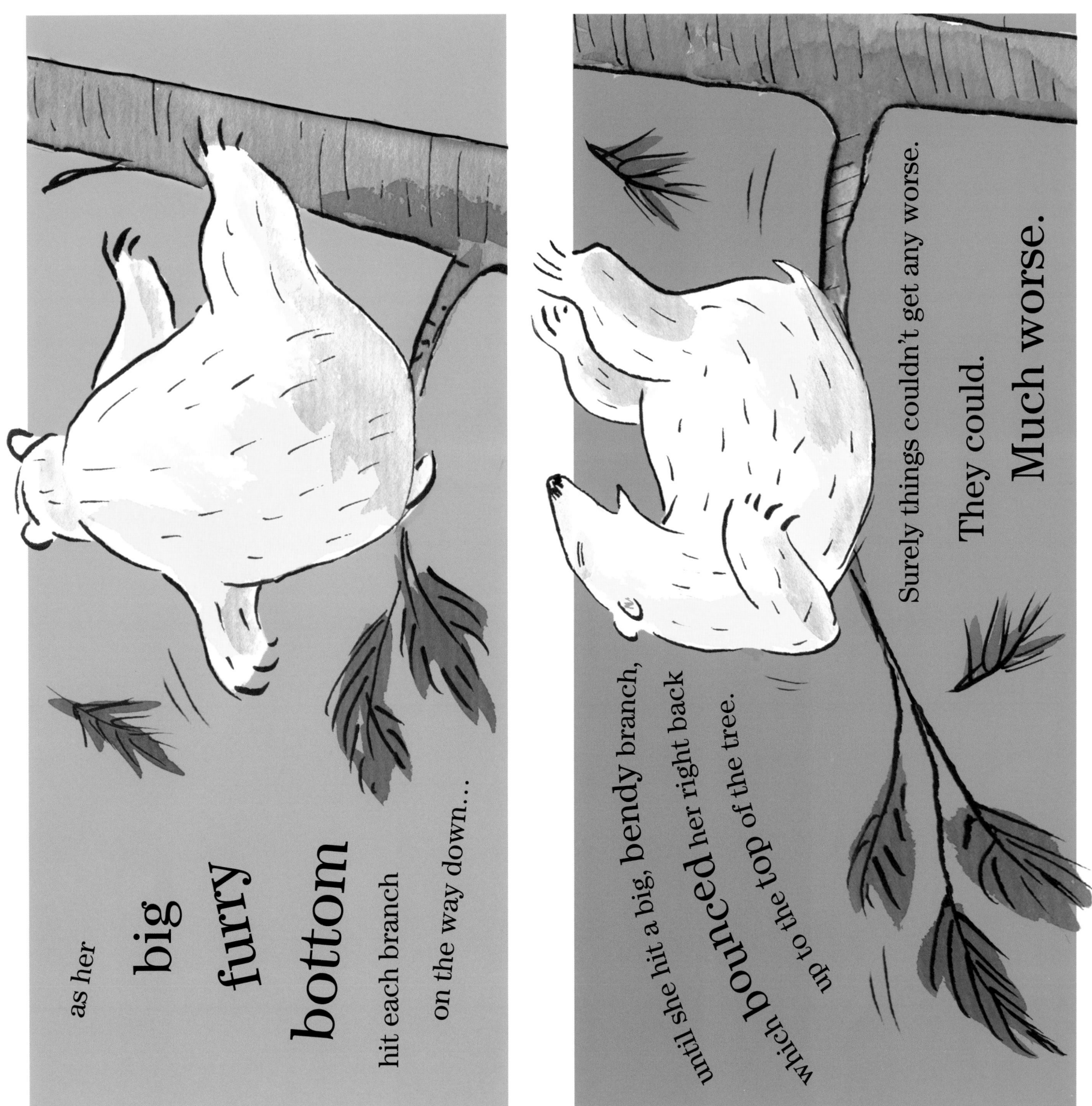

as her **big furry bottom** hit each branch on the way down...

until she hit a big, bendy branch, which **bounced** her right back up to the top of the tree.

Surely things couldn't get any worse.

They could.

Much worse.

As the polar bear was so heavy, the tree buckled to one side. The pack of brown bears reached up with their paws and grabbed at the trunk.

"Get the **BOOGIE MONSTER!**" ordered the little one.

The brown bears lost their **grip** on the trunk,
and the tree **twanged** back up.

Twong!

A twong is like a twang but more twongy.

"**Oooohhh dddeeaarrr!**"

screamed the polar bear as she soared through the air.

"It's a flying **BOOGIE MONSTER!**"

remarked the one with the biggest, wettest nose.

Now polar bears are not natural fliers. None have wings or own jet-packs or can pilot helicopters...

In no time the poor animal had crash-landed headfirst into a **huge** muddy puddle.

Splat!

...If you think you have seen a polar bear flying a helicopter, please consult a doctor.

"A BOOGIE BEAR!" shouted the littlest one.

A huge smile spread across the face of the one with the floppy ears.

"She's not a **BOOGIE** ANYTHING. She's gorgeous."

"Boring!" fumed the littlest one.

"Miss, we are so sorry for frightening you,"
said the one with the floppy ears, stepping forward.
"In truth, we were frightened. Here, you see,
all us bears are brown."

"There all us bears are white,"
she said, pointing north.

"I love your **white** fur,"

said the **brown** bear, checking out
the white bear's big, furry **bottom**.

"I love your **brown** fur,"

said the **white** bear, checking out
the brown bear's big, furry **bottom**.

"Yuckety yuck
yuck
yuck!"

exclaimed the
littlest one.

The pair rubbed **noses** in a show of **love**. The birds in the trees tweeted sweet music, butterflies swooped and twirled and, as if that wasn't enough, a **rainbow** appeared in the sky.

From that day on, the two lovestruck bears spent **all** their days and nights together.

The white bear had never eaten **honey** before, which she **loved**.
The brown bear had never eaten **walrus** before,
which he **pretended** to love.

🐾 I would not recommend eating
walrus. You have to smother it with
tomato ketchup to make it taste nice.

The pair hibernated for the winter,
cuddled up together
in a hollowed-out tree.

Things couldn't get any better.

But they could.

Much better . . .

That spring, the polar bear had a litter of **beautiful bear cubs.**

Their **fur** came in lots of different shades of **white**
and **brown**. No matter, their mummy and
daddy loved them **all** the same.

"This **really** is the life!" sighed the **white** bear.
"It certainly **is**, my love," replied the
brown bear.